THIS CANDLEWICK BOOK BELONGS TO:

_____

_____

_____

_____

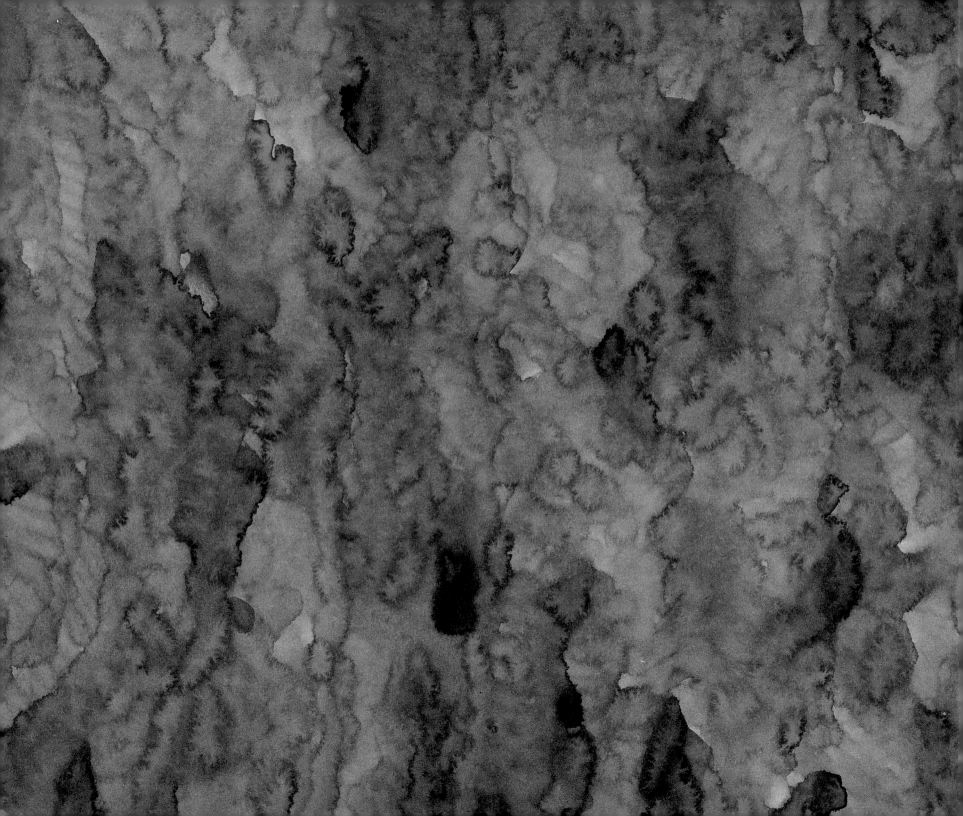

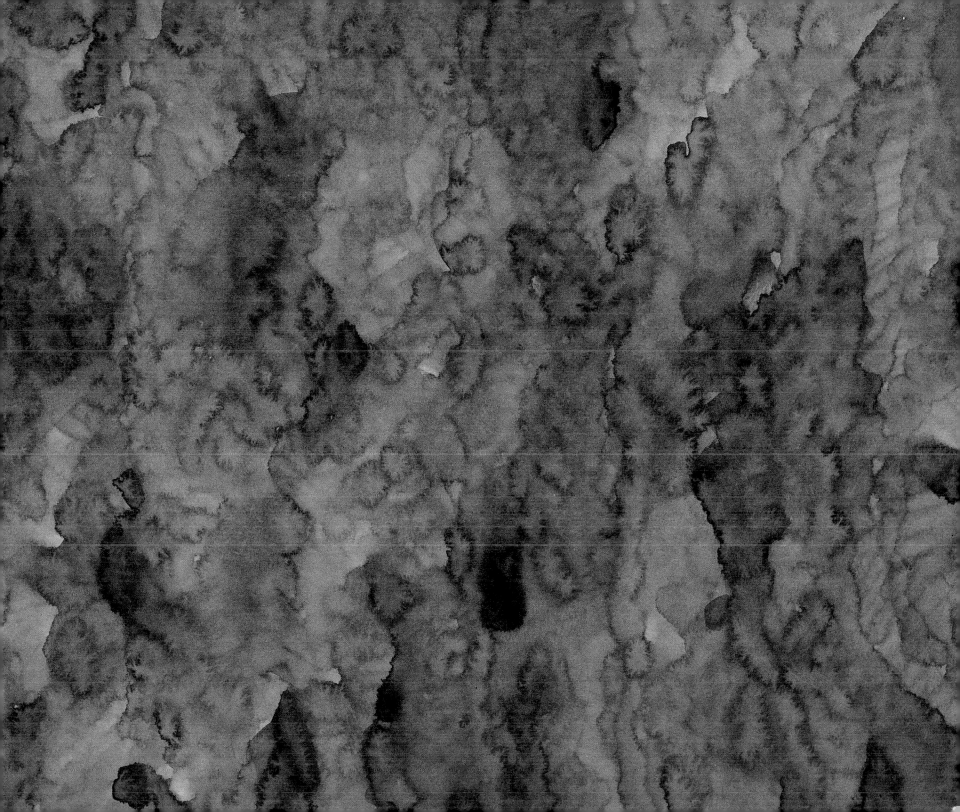

Copyright © 1993 by Jan Ormerod

First U.S. paperback edition 1995

Library of Congress Cataloging-in-Publication Data
Ormerod, Jan
Midnight pillow fight / Jan Ormerod.—1st U.S. ed.
Summary: A young girl engages in a midnight romp with
pillows from around the house.
ISBN 1-56402-169-6 (hardcover)—1-56402-520-9 (paperback)
[1. Pillows—Fiction. 2. Bedtime—Fiction.] I. Title.
PZ7.O634Mi   1993                                92-53011
[E]–dc20

2 4 6 8 10 9 7 5 3 1

Printed in Hong Kong

The pictures in this book were done in
watercolor and pen and ink.

Candlewick Press
2067 Massachusetts Avenue
Cambridge, Massachusetts 02140

Jan Ormerod
# MIDNIGHT PILLOW FIGHT

## CANDLEWICK PRESS
### CAMBRIDGE, MASSACHUSETTS

Have *you* ever woken up in the middle of the night?

Have *you* ever had a midnight pillow fight?     Polly has . . .

and look how it started.

Polly thought her pillow was alive.

She thought it wanted to play.

Has *your* pillow ever wanted to play in the middle of the night?

Polly's has.

Look, they went downstairs on tiptoe.

Polly peeked and what did she see?

Some cushions were awake too.

For a moment Polly stood
and watched.

I wonder what she felt, don't you?

This is how Polly said hello.

And this is how they played.

Now where did these big cushions come from?

Have *you* ever marched and danced like this,

having lots of fun in the middle of the night?

Look, they played leapfrog. Up and over . . . up and over . . .

up and over!

BUMP!

Oh, poor pillow!

Polly pushed – would *you* do that?

Polly got ready to fight.

Ready, steady . . . WHOOSH!

WALLOP! WHOOSH! WHOP!

WHOOSH! WHOP! WALLOP! *"Please stop!"* Polly turned on the light.

And the pillow fight stopped.

Polly put the cushions

back in their places.

Everything was still again.

Polly took her pillow up to bed.

Why do you think she looked so sad?

Have *you* ever hugged your pillow in the middle of the night? Polly has.

And look! All the cushions came upstairs to see if Polly was all right.

Have *you* ever woken up in the middle of the night? Have *you* ever

had a midnight pillow fight? Polly has... and this is how it ended.

JAN ORMEROD, an award-winning author-illustrator, is well known as the creator of *Sunshine, Dad's Back,* and many other books for children. When she began *Midnight Pillow Fight,* it was wordless. "I always conceive of a whole book as if it were a film, a continuous flow of action," she explains. "Then I choose moments to stop the film, and write text later." For this story, she tried to imagine what an adult and child might say to each other while looking at the book.